Harvey the Gardener

Lars Klinting

KINGFISHER

The plant on Harvey's windowsill has wilted. It looks terrible! He'll have to get a new one. What kind should he buy?

Harvey can't decide . . .
But wait! What are those
little white things rolling
across the floor?

Harvey follows the trail and finds Chip!

Chip has been shopping, but he had too much to carry.

He dropped the bag of white beans that Harvey planned to cook for lunch, and they have rolled everywhere.

It's all right, though - it's given Harvey an idea!

That's it! He'll grow beans on the windowsill.
Hurrah!

That evening, Harvey puts the beans they are going to plant into a little bowl of water – one, two, three, four, five, six, seven, eight, nine, ten!

Harvey explains that beans grow faster if
they soak over night. Then he goes to bed.
Chip is too excited to sleep!

The next morning Harvey and Chip go into the garden shed. They are searching for something . . .

Here it is! Clever Chip! It was on the shelf all along.

Harvey's gardening book will tell them everything they need to know about growing beans.

a small trowel

two broken bits
of pot that are
called crocks

and a bag of potting compost.

Harvey covers the hole in the bottom of each pot with one of the crocks so that the compost won't fall out.

Then he fills the pots with the compost.
See if there's any left in the bag, Chip!

Now Harvey fetches the soaked beans. They are almost twice as big as they were before!

Next he sharpens a stick and draws a red line on it.

Harvey pokes the stick into each pot three times, to make three holes in the soil. He pushes the stick right down to the red line to make sure the holes will be deep enough.

Chip drops a bean into each hole and covers it with soil. But hold on – three beans in each pot makes six. There are four beans left! Don't worry, Chip.

Harvey has a plan.

Now they need a watering can!

Chip fills it up and sprinkles the pots with water.

Not too much, Chip, or the beans will drown!

While Chip is busy watering, Harvey sneaks outside with the leftover beans. He plants them in a flowerbed next to the wall, where it is sunny and warm.

Chip can't wait for the beans to grow.
At first, nothing happens. He waters
and watches and waits for nearly
a whole week. Then one morning,
just when he's nearly ready to
give up . . .

Look what's happened! Chip is so excited!

All three of his beans have grown into little plants.
In Harvey's pot, only two have come up.

Harvey fetches some bamboo sticks from the shed.
Carefully, he and Chip push them into the pots.

Now the beans have something to climb while they grow.

Every day they water the pots. The plants grow and grow . . .

. . . and grow, until the whole window is filled with leaves. Harvey is thrilled to see the beautiful flowers, but Chip is more excited by the beans!

Together they pick the longest,
fattest bean-pods.

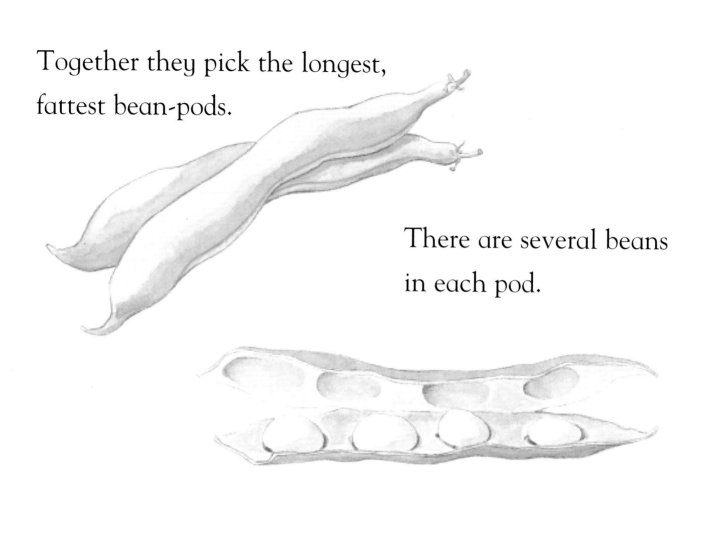

There are several beans
in each pod.

The beans have tough
white skins but inside
they are bright green.

Together, Harvey and Chip wash and peel the beans.
It's not easy to take off those tough white skins!
At last they are finished and the beans are ready to
cook. Into the water they go, with a little salt.

They boil them for a couple of minutes, then drain
them and put the warm beans on plates. Harvey
adds butter to make them even nicer.

What a big reward from six little beans - beautiful plants on the windowsill all summer and then a feast as well!

But look, Chip.
What's growing over there in the flowerbed?

Wow! There are beans growing outside, too!

Chip has no idea where they've come from –
and Harvey doesn't tell him. Now they can
have beans tomorrow, too! Yummy!

Harvey's Gardening Tips

White bean

Brown bean

Black bean

Black-eyed bean

Pinto bean

Kidney bean

Dried white beans, like the ones Chip bought for dinner, are easy to grow. They grow very quickly, too. You can try to grow other kinds of beans. Beans are really seeds, and in seed-shops there are even more kinds to choose from.

Spring is the best time to plant, since beans need a lot of light and warmth. But you can plant beans indoors at any time of year. The beans might not be as large and tasty, but it's exciting to watch them grow.

One little tip is to plant your beans in a hole that's twice as big as the bean. That's true for almost all other seeds as well. You mustn't forget to water them! But remember, not too little and not too much. The soil should always be damp. If you water too much, the roots may rot. That's why it's good to have the little hole in the bottom of the pot. All the excess water can drain out through there.

Dried beans are really hard and must be cooked for a long time before they can be eaten. But fresh beans are so soft that it only takes a couple of minutes before they're ready. However, you can't plant fresh beans. You have to wait until they're ripe and hard. Then the little bean contains everything that is necessary for it to sprout roots (germinate) and grow.

You can leave some bean-pods on the stalk to ripen and dry. Later in the autumn you can collect the beans and store them indoors. The beans must be kept dry during the winter. When it's spring again, you can soak the beans and plant them in pots or in the ground. The beans germinate and everything starts all over again...

The
End